The Ebony Duckling

First printing

PUBLISHED BY WINSTON-DEREK PUBLISHERS, INC.
Nashville, Tennessee 37205

Library of Congress Catalog Card No: 90-75090
ISBN: 1-55523-457-7

Printed in the United States of America

For Blue

THE MOTHER DUCK SAT ON HER EGGS

The Ebony Duckling

Retold from a Hans Christian Andersen story
by Fred Crump Jr.

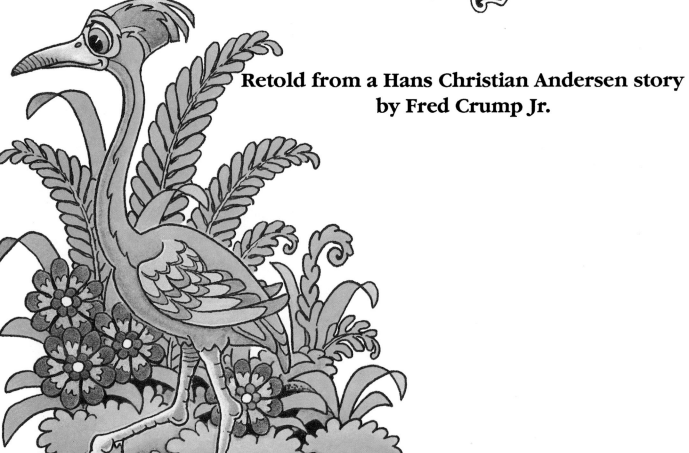

At the edge of a pond in a farm yard, a mother duck sat on her nest. Many days passed. Then, at last, one day came the sound of cracking egg shells and little peeps.

A shell cracked open, and there sat a cute fuzzy little golden duckling.

"Quack!" it said.

Then a second little duckling popped out of its shell.

"Quack!" it said.

"Handsome children," said the father duck, fluffing up his chest feathers.

TWO BEAUTIFUL BABY DUCKS

The third egg took a little longer, but at last it cracked open. And there sat an ebony raggedy looking little fellow.

"Honk," he said.

"Oh my!" said mother duck.

"Oh no!" said father duck, "I think maybe a turkey egg got in our nest by mistake. That is too different to be a duck."

Now although he was brand new, the ebony duckling could tell that this was *not* a good beginning.

"Maybe a big crow?" mumbled father duck, "or a penguin?" He waddled off quacking to himself.

"Time for a swim," said mother duck. "All three of you, into the water."

...AND ONE SURPRISE

The ebony duckling loved the water. He paddled and splashed and swam in circles and tried to impress the mother duck. But she ignored him and gave all her attention to the other two ducklings.

"Go find another mother," said one little duck.

"Go live with the turkeys," said the other little duck.

They nagged and splashed and squirted water on him until he climbed out of the pond.

NOT A GOOD BEGINNING

The ebony duckling wandered off into the farm yard. He saw a mother goose with two little goslings.

"Say," he said to the goose. "I don't guess you would maybe like to have an extra left-over kid?"

"You?" said the goose. "Oh my, no! My family is large enough. Please go away."

So the ebony duckling sadly trudged on.

THE MOTHER GOOSE SAID "NO"

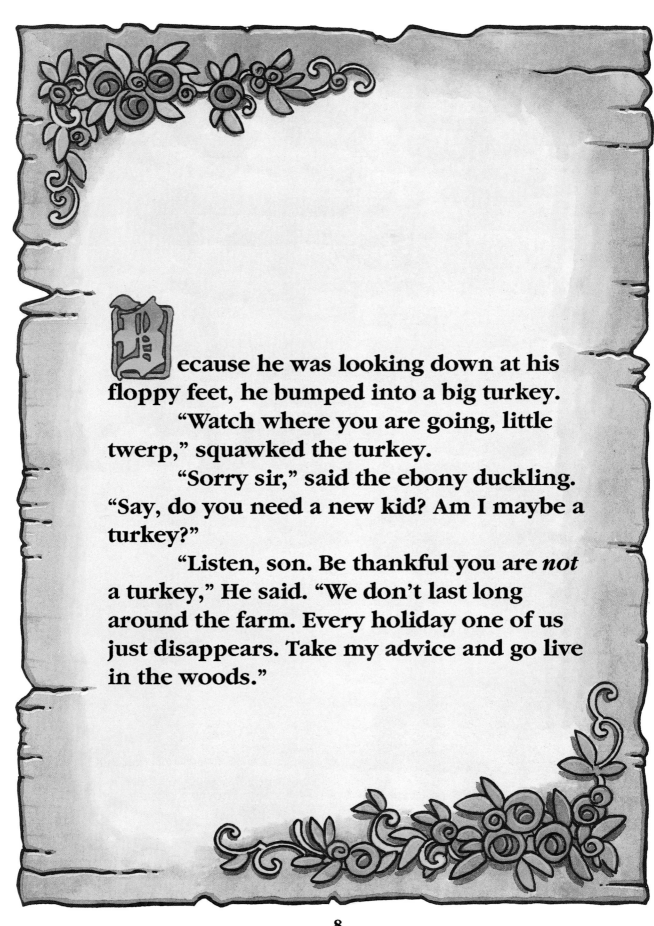

ecause he was looking down at his floppy feet, he bumped into a big turkey.

"Watch where you are going, little twerp," squawked the turkey.

"Sorry sir," said the ebony duckling. "Say, do you need a new kid? Am I maybe a turkey?"

"Listen, son. Be thankful you are *not* a turkey," He said. "We don't last long around the farm. Every holiday one of us just disappears. Take my advice and go live in the woods."

THE TURKEY WAS A GROUCH

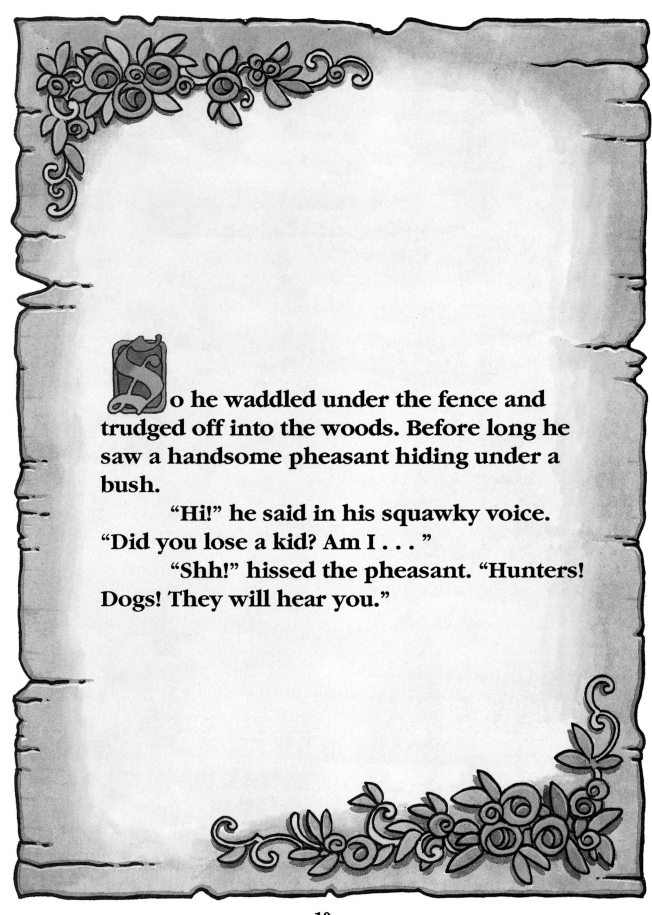

So he waddled under the fence and trudged off into the woods. Before long he saw a handsome pheasant hiding under a bush.

"Hi!" he said in his squawky voice. "Did you lose a kid? Am I . . . "

"Shh!" hissed the pheasant. "Hunters! Dogs! They will hear you."

THE PHEASANT WAS HIDING

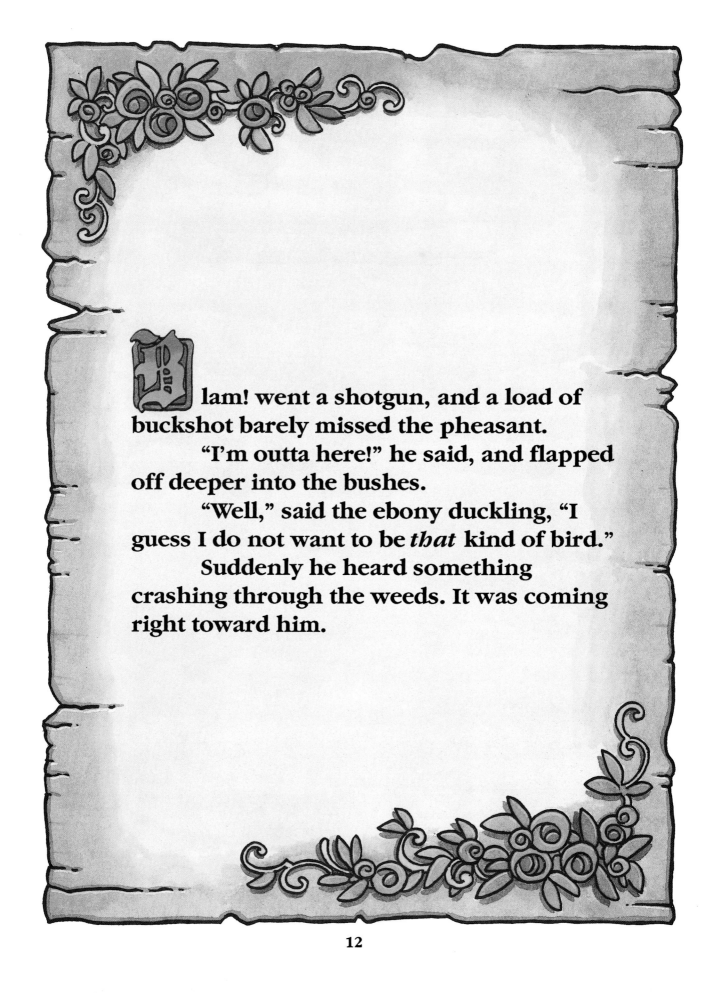

lam! went a shotgun, and a load of buckshot barely missed the pheasant.

"I'm outta here!" he said, and flapped off deeper into the bushes.

"Well," said the ebony duckling, "I guess I do not want to be *that* kind of bird."

Suddenly he heard something crashing through the weeds. It was coming right toward him.

PHEASANT HUNTERS

He tried to hide in the tall grass. Then right above him a big old hound dog poked his head through the weeds and looked all around.

The ebony duckling was too scared to wiggle even a feather. At last the hunter called the dog and he trotted away.

"I sure could use a mommy about now," whimpered the little duck. "This is no fun!"

HIDING FROM A HOUND DOG

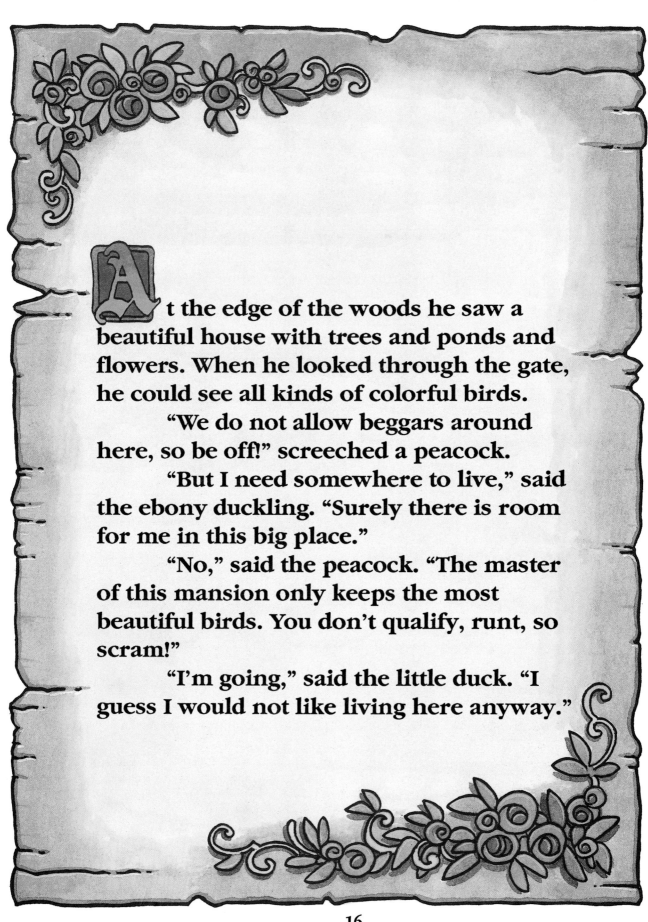

At the edge of the woods he saw a beautiful house with trees and ponds and flowers. When he looked through the gate, he could see all kinds of colorful birds.

"We do not allow beggars around here, so be off!" screeched a peacock.

"But I need somewhere to live," said the ebony duckling. "Surely there is room for me in this big place."

"No," said the peacock. "The master of this mansion only keeps the most beautiful birds. You don't qualify, runt, so scram!"

"I'm going," said the little duck. "I guess I would not like living here anyway."

THE PEACOCK TOLD HIM TO GO AWAY

The ebony duckling wandered back into the woods. He got hooted at by an owl, burped at by a bull frog and chased by a fox.

He ran lickety-split into a hollow log and the fox tried to crawl in after him.

LOOKING FOR A PLACE TO HIDE

ut the fox could only get his head in, so after awhile he went off to chase something else.

"I don't think I'm having fun yet," said the little duck. "Well, I only have one place left to go."

So he went back to the pond to his old nest. He gathered up the pieces of his egg shell. Then he tried to put it all together so he could crawl back in.

BACK TO THE NEST

ut it just didn't work. The shell kept falling apart.

Then a kind voice said, "Hello, little swan, are you having trouble?"

The ebony duckling looked up to see an elegant bird with a long graceful neck and welcoming wings.

"Swan?" he said. "Me? Is this a joke?"

The mother swan put a comforting wing around him.

"It is no joke, if you are alone, you can be another one of my children. Meet your new brother and sister."

And two baby swans gave him a warm welcome greeting.

IS THiS A JOKE ?

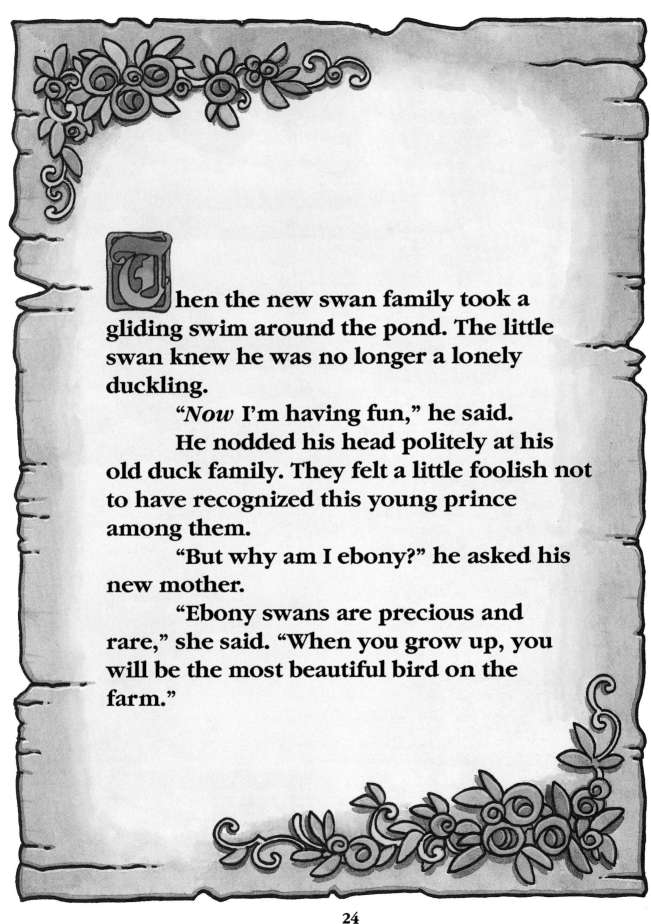

hen the new swan family took a gliding swim around the pond. The little swan knew he was no longer a lonely duckling.

"*Now* I'm having fun," he said.

He nodded his head politely at his old duck family. They felt a little foolish not to have recognized this young prince among them.

"But why am I ebony?" he asked his new mother.

"Ebony swans are precious and rare," she said. "When you grow up, you will be the most beautiful bird on the farm."

HELLO TO THE DUCKS

And indeed he was.